The Elfree Stories

Written and Illustrated by

Anne Muller

&

Elfree of the Leaf

Published in 2001 by
The Collins Press
West Link Park
Doughcloyne
Wilton
Cork

British Library Cataloguing in Publication data.

Typesetting by Artmark.

Printed by Estudios Gráficos Zure, S.A. – Bilbao (Spain)

ISBN: 1-903464-056

Letters from
an Irish grandmother
to her Australian grandchildren
with stories told to her
by Elfree of the Leaf

Dedicated to
Zandy, Diana, Liam & Andy

Dear children

While I was walking in the Woods today I came upon an elf. He looked a bit surprised when he realised I could see him, but he quickly recovered and took off his hat and bowed to me. He told me his name was Elfree of the Leaf. I replied that I was Gran of the Muller-Yelens and that seemed to please him.

He had never actually spoken to a human before and I had to answer a lot of questions, but he particularly wanted to know about you; and as we sat on a log overlooking the Bay he told me a story for you. It is partly true, partly fiction and partly just fun. It also has a beginning, a middle and an end; and is about courage, kindness and cats; which makes it very much a three-part story.

Did you know that cats were once terribly clumsy, ungainly creatures? Well, according to Elfree, they were dreadful bumblers, always tripping over their own paws. Here is the story as it was told to me by Elfree in his own words.

"It started," said Elfree, "around about June.
The nights feeling warmer; round was the moon.
It silvered the gorse and shadowed the bay.
It lit up the woods and brightened our way.
We were all there, we nocturnal sprites,
Dancing and singing long into the night,
When suddenly, who should stomp into our throng?
But a cat with a tail at least a foot long!
Now rabbits we know, and like them quite well,
Also squirrels and mice and other folk of the dell,
But cats; they have claws and eyes that burn green
And when in a temper they hiss and they scream.

So a terrible silence
greeted that cat,
Except for a small elf,
who bravely said 'Scat!'
His mother then grabbing him up with a frown
Tucked him away in the folds of her gown.
That's when I asked, in a voice small and low,
What that cat wanted, or needed to know?
'I've come to your gathering to learn how to dance,'
Said the cat, scratching his ear with a claw like a lance.
'We felines are clumsy and slow and ungainly,
Some even say stupid, though very unfairly.
So I've come here to learn how to leap and to prance.
In short, will you please teach me to dance?'
At this all the sprites took three paces back.
How on Earth could we teach that great hairy sack
To turn and to gambol, to frolic and skip,
When all he could do was trundle and trip?
'How can we teach such an ungainly beast
To dance?' said an imp from a tree out of reach.
At that the poor cat turned away with a sigh
And a great glittery tear dropped from his eye.
'You're right,' said the cat. 'It was selfish, I see,
To ask graceful sprites to spend time teaching me.
My paws are too big and my tail is too long,
My eyes are quite squint and I know
I'm all wrong.'

I'll teach you to dance,' said a
kind little fairy.
'I'll teach you to dance and feel
graceful and airy,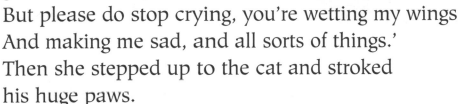
But please do stop crying, you're wetting my wings
And making me sad, and all sorts of things.'
Then she stepped up to the cat and stroked
his huge paws.
'Now first you must learn how to retract your claws.
Then I shall ask the Wizard of Ravity
To teach you to defy the law of gravity.'
Then all of us knew we would try, and keep trying,
Until that clumsy cat danced as though he was flying;
And that's what we did for a year and a day;
Now all cats are graceful, at sleep and at play.
No cat is now called a clumsy old beast
And at the end of it all we had a great feast."

Perhaps we should suggest to
aunt Jo-Anne that she teach our
cats to sing. Even I, a great
admirer of how graceful and
beautiful cats are, have to admit
that they have awful voices.

Love,

Gran

Dear children

Today I found Elfree sitting sadly on a stone wall. I asked him why he was so glum and he showed me his hat; it was all scrunched and the feather was broken. Of course I knew that elves love their hats and that Elfree was very proud of his, so I understood his gloomy mood. I offered to make him a new hat.

You know me, I had it made in no time at all and added a sparkling brooch to pin on the new feather; just for fun.

Well Elfree was delighted and said it was better than his first hat and that he would never leave it in a place where farmer O'Connor's great muddy cows could stand on it. Then, of course, I knew what had happened to his crumpled hat.

I told him you had enjoyed his story, so he told me another. As he said, it is a serious story, sad at the start but happy at the end.

"There are many sad things in this world, as you know,
Like very fast things that have to go slow
And air so polluted that snowfalls in the night
Turn the world grey and not sparkling white.
Like puppies and kittens with no children around
And things that get lost and never are found.
Like children with parents too busy to play
Or grandparents who live too far away.
But one of the saddest things. Do you know?
Is a faun in the forest who can't make things grow.
An elf who can't paint is among the sad things
And a fairy who gets tangled up in her wings
And, believe me, no drama in life makes me cry
Like a bee who is simply too tired to fly.
But bees, elves or fairies, snow, kittens or dogs;
Nothing's so sad as a forlorn faun in the bogs;
For bogs will stay bleak till the fauns grow the trees
That give shelter to everyone, from people to bees.
And this is where the serious part
Of my story about a sad faun starts.
The name that was given to this little faun
On the night following the day he was born
Was *Silvergreen of Pine-Forest and Fir*
And one day he'd inherit the grand title of *sir*,
For he came from a family, wise and old,
Who grew trees in climates both warm and cold,
For, as everyone knows, who has travelled there,
Fir trees and pine trees grow everywhere.

When Silvergreen was only three
He was given his own little fir tree
And was told to care for it and make it grow
Through spring and summer and before winter's snow.
So Silvergreen cared for his little fir,
Planting it, weeding it, and making sure
That it was clean and warm and watered well
And out of the wind down in the dell.
But all that spring and summer and fall
That little fir tree did not grow at all,
Not one tiny shoot or small spiky leaf,
It stayed the same, to the little faun's grief.
Now the oldest faun shook his head
And gave him a weed to look after instead.

The snow came down soon after the fall
And a soft white blanket covered all
And, free to play till the springtime came,
The fauns danced patterns in the snow,
a favourite game.
But Silvergreen sat on a stone,
A sad little figure, all on his own.
'Why can't I grow things like other fauns do?
Even my weed has gone down with the "flu".'
'Now cheer up lad,' said a friendly elf.
'Tell me what's wrong, perhaps I can help.'
So the faun told his tale to his new-found friend
And the elf said, 'That's simple, your gloom's at an end.
If you want to make sure little things grow,
There is something important you have to know.
Love them and laugh with them, then you will see
How your little sapling becomes a tree."

I've always been very fond of fauns and I'm glad
this faun got such good advice from his friend.

Love,

Gran

Dear children

Today our little elfin friend came right into the house and sat on my art table on an upturned box with the feather on his hat bobbing up and down as he spoke. Of course, being an elf, he didn't sit all the time. Most of the time he was skipping around among my paints, leaving more than a few coloured footprints on my papers. Again he wanted to hear all about you and, because I'm always ready to talk about my wonderful grandchildren, we had a long chat. A very pleasant chat too, although, when I told him you could shout, and pretty crossly sometimes, he nearly fell off his box. He then asked me to write this letter to you as elfin writing looks something like this

and none of us could possibly read it.

"I'm watching your grandmother's pen move along.
Elves use runes that flow like a song
But your grandmother says you can't read that way
So I'll have to use words in this letter today.
Annie says you are aged between one and seven,
That's not very old if you are elfin.
She says you all have lovely smiles,
To elves that is precious and most worthwhile.
I'm told when you're cross you can shout very loudly
And, although I'm as brave as a lion, that is scary,
For to elfin ears a cross shout's like a bellow
And can turn an elf from leaf green to yellow
And that's how we stay for the rest of the day,
Yellow and droopy and unwilling to play.
But I'm told when you're happy your voices are low,
Like a kitten's soft purring and waters that flow,
And your laughter and singing's a wonderful sound
That makes everyone happy for elf miles* around.
I hope, for the sake of Australian sprites,
You sing more than you shout and laugh
more than you fight.
Trees love to hear music, we sing to them here.
If you listen I'm sure you'll hear elves singing there,
But I wanted to tell you a story so old
That old elves can't remember when first it was told.

* Elves' hearing is far more acute than that of humans.

Some say it goes back to before the ice age
And was told to the elves by an old human sage.
For in those days men and elves
saw each other quite clearly
And most elves liked people,
and some loved them dearly.
But back to my story of the age before ice,
Before horses and John's cows and beavers and mice.
When great stags roamed through
the ancient old forests
And the gentlest beasts known were
the silver-backed sorrets:
They were little horses with tiny wings
And silver backs and golden rings
Which they wore on their tails
to keep them neat
And small ebony hooves
at the ends of their feet.
We elves loved the sorrets and rode them like you,
Who ride their descendants and love them too.

We flew and we galloped and played in the forests
And groomed the silver hair on the backs of our sorrets.
There was, at that time, a harp of great beauty;
With a sound when men played it of such rare purity
That the angels would leave their heavenly places
To listen with men and all fairy races.
There are ancient old elves from the green ferny glen

Who say they still have that harp from
the old world of men
But, as elves are too light to make it play,
It's been silent since that terrible day:
That terrible day that the wizard of Dirth
Came over to Ireland with a boatload of serfs.
He left his own land, wild, treeless and cold
And sailed over to Ireland, or so I've been told

And the first thing he did, that terrible Dirth,
Was to cut down our trees and plough up the earth,
Then the men of old Ireland started doing it too
And we elfin creatures could just not get through
To those men with their saws and axes so sharp
So we left and went south, carrying Ireland's great harp.
The sorrets, they stayed, and grew big on the pastures

But they lost their wings when they
gained their new masters.
For the wizard of Dirth simply hated to fly
And he punished his serfs if they wanted to try.
From that time to this elves still cannot get through
To men, or seldom, and then only a few
And some say, the sage said, that's how it would stay
Till the great harp of Ireland is heard
once more to play".

"Let's go for a walk," said Elfree then.
I looked out of the window at the rain.
"This is what we elves call a feathery day,
The flurries of rain and the trees so grey,
Making lacy patterns against the sky."
So up into the hills went the elf and I.
Over the rocks and through the heather,
Walking in Elfree's feathery weather.
And thinking of you in the Australian sun,
Although walks in the mist can also be fun.

Love,

Gran

Dear children

There are things about Elfree that remind me of you. He does ask a lot of questions that are very hard to answer, especially when I'm concentrating on painting; although his questions are about things that puzzle an elf and yours are about things that puzzle children.

You know how he sits on a box on my art table? Well today it went like this: –

"Why do you walk so slowly up hills?
Why do you keep these plants on your sills?
Why do you wear those things on your nose?
What makes you want to paint a wild rose?
Do all grandmothers complain about the rain
And hum the same tune over and over again?
Why do men plant trees in such straight rows?
Do you really think you've captured that rose?
Why can't you climb a tree with me
And sit in its branches so that we can see
The valley below all misty and grey?

Why can't you stop working so we can play?
Why are humans so busy?" Elfree sighed.
"You ask too many questions," I replied.
"I really can't talk to you when I paint,"
I said, smiling at Elfree looking so quaint
In his hat and his jacket and bright red socks
In the middle of my table on his upturned box.
"You tell me all about elves," I said
"And I'll listen to you talking instead."

"We elves are the thinkers of the fairy races;
Music and dance are our two main graces,
But we do spend time thinking, when we're at home,
Then we pass on our thoughts
to the dwarves and gnomes;
For they make things happen
and give most things names
And that leaves us free to get on with our games.
I could teach you an elf game," he added brightly
"But you'll have to learn to be a bit more sprightly.
Elves are not always as small as me,
Some elves can grow to six foot three.
It all depends on how large our space is
And the genealogy of the different races.
We think story-telling is one of the arts
And, as you know, they have three or four parts.
Our listeners though, must unravel the mystery
Of whether they are fiction, or part of our history.

I like to think elves are the best," said he,
"But there are some times, I must agree,
That we are not all that gracious, or even friendly
And we could at times be much more kindly.
But then there are times
when we're proud of ourselves,
Like the time the storm goblin was helped by us elves.
I tell you this story with some hesitation
For it's about a goblin that came
from an Australian station;
A goblin so mean and ugly in form
That wherever he went he took his own storm.
Now storm goblins like this are so horrid and hairy,
So nasty and bad and frightfully scary,
That we were told never to talk to one
Especially during a setting sun.
Be warned never to look them in the eye
And if you do be sure to cry
So the image is washed clear away
Or he'll turn you to ice for many a day.
So, if you meet one, look right through him
As if you never even knew him!"

"I know," I said. "You don't alarm me,
We have men like that in the army."
"What's an army?" he said. "Tell me that story."
"It's something men join for king and glory.
I'll tell you later, first go on with your story
Of the horrible goblin, ugly and stormy."
"Well our elders made it very clear
That, if we met one, we should show no fear,
For fear's what they eat. It makes them fat.
So never show fear, they starve on that.
Well one day this goblin from the station,
And I recall this part with trepidation,
Came stumbling into our spring gathering
With a snorty roar that set us shivering
And just as we were preparing to run
The goblin said, 'Stop please, I just wanted some fun.
Everyone's always so frightened of me
And that makes the storm so much worse, you see?
I put on weight till I'm as heavy as lead.
I know goblins don't die but I wish I was dead.'
Then kindness and courtesy and our good graces
Leaped up in our hearts and showed on our faces.

We asked what we could do to assist our new friend,
To help bring his woes and his pain to an end.
'Well you could all join hands in a ring around me
And sing out loud that you quite like me.'
So 'round we danced and sang his praises
In elfin tones and elfin phrases

Till at last he shouted out with pleasure,
'I feel like air, just like a feather!'
We elfin folk became his brothers
And so, might I add, did many others.
We have never seen storm goblins again.
They won't come near our elfin glen.
They're afraid they'll lose their goblin powers
And end up happily planting flowers."

So there you are my darlings. Now we know what to do with storm goblins that may bumble into our lives.

Love,

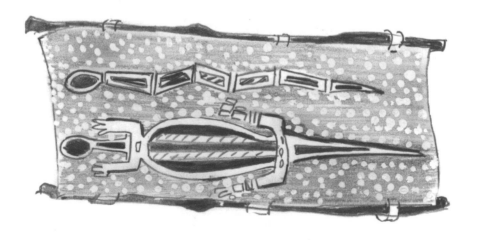

Dear children

Yesterday I told Elfree about the deer I had seen in the woods and he went off to find them.

Today he told me how he had followed their footprints through the heather and gorse with a friend of his and he ended his story with:

> "Finally my hob-goblin friend and I
> Saw the two deer passing by.
> I hope they like it here and stay
> And never want to go away!"

I listened to his story and I was surprised that he was playing with a hob-goblin and I said "I thought you hated hob goblins and the way they play."

Then my little elf friend looked at me aghast ...

"Don't use that word, it's from the past!
A terrible word, too awful to say.
Now we'll have to clear it away,
For it hovers around darkening the place.
Oh! There are things about the human race
That are so difficult to understand.
Don't sit looking surprised, I need a hand!"
"What can I do," I asked my elf,
For I could see he was beside himself.
"Words are powerful. Don't you know?
They have their own colours, music and glow
And some ancient words are never said;
They fill the place with fear and dread.
They're black, and can hurt most painfully,
Much better that they never be
Let loose into the atmosphere
To absorb the light and pollute the air.
Better to say, 'I do not like'
Than fill the room with painful spikes.
Please help me clear that word away.
It's becoming too painful for me to stay."

"What can I do?" I asked again,
"I'm very sorry I caused you pain."
"Listen to me while I sing
And think of roses in the spring,
Of saphires blue and sunlit waters,
Of the love you feel for your sons and daughters,
Of the children that you love so much,
Of Diana's laugh and Zandy's touch,
And I will sing an elfin song;
If you help me now it won't take long."
So I sat and thought of beautiful things
And Elfree's song gave my thoughts wings;
A beautiful song that I think I've heard
In happy places where love is shared,
In the talking of golden autumn leaves
And grasses moving in the breeze.
In a pine-cone fire on a winter's night
Or when children's voices are full of delight.
Daddy's heard it too, when the wind blows free
And his sail-board's flying across the sea;
Mummy hears it when she takes a peep
To check on you when you're asleep.

We hear it when Liam and Andy smile
And, if you listen for a while,
You'll hear it too; it's all around you,
In so many things that surround you.
When the song had come to an end
I asked my little elfin friend
If the room was again bright and clear
And if he was more comfortable in here,
And if there were other words I must not say,
As I did not like to upset him that way.
"Oh! You know what words make people sad?
Well those are the words that elves find bad."
And he grinned at me from his upturned box,
In his new green hat and bright red socks
And told me a tale about reputations;
Which is very important in elfin nations,
But, although I thought the story a winner,
I have to go now to cook the dinner.
    Love,

Gran

Dear children,

Today Elfree told me a story about
reputation, pride and frogs.

"Elves care a lot about their reputation,
For themselves and for their nation,
And even young elves know they should
    Give folk a reputation that is good;
For reputation is what you
    leave behind you
And paves the way that lies before you.
    And life is easier," said the elf,
    "For other folk and for yourself
    If all the good things that folk do
    Are well spoken of and
        remembered too.
    So we feel reputation
        deserves protection

And, if sometimes it needs correction,
We try to do it very quickly,
That way life is much less prickly."

"This is a tale of a frog at the age
Where he'd just grown out of the tadpole stage
And he found himself, as most frogs do,
At the edge of a pond, deep and blue.
This little frog was handsome and green
And as he sat on a stump, surveying the scene,
He saw a sulky old trout being teased by
A swiftly darting dragonfly
And various other flying things
With the sun shining brightly in their wings.
He saw a fork-tailed swallow flying fast,
Skimming the water as it flew past

And a butterfly settling softly down
On a water lily's golden crown.
He saw a beaver building a dam of logs
But what interested him most were the other frogs.
A noisy lot, they flopped about,
Rippling the water and scaring the trout.
Leaping from one lily-pad to another,
Croaking and jumping and splashing each other.
They seemed to be having a lot of fun
As they played in the pond in the summer sun;
Then he heard a frog quite close to him say,
'Let's see who can leap the farthest today.'
And onto the beaver's dam of logs
Scrambled a group of eager frogs.
They jumped into the pond, one by one,
Then an old frog said, 'Your turn son.'
No one noticed that the little frog had
Jumped no distance at all, but he felt bad.
So he climbed back up onto his stump
And would not try another jump.

Too proud to lose, he felt ashamed
And wouldn't play any more games.
As the summer changed to early fall
Our frog grew bigger, but he still felt small,
So he sat alone and never joined in,
He would not play if he could not win.
'The games are silly and stupid,' he'd say,
When other frogs asked him to play.
And so he got the reputation
Of saying 'no' to every invitation,
Until, one day while he was watching
A competition of long distance jumping,
A smelly monster came bounding up;
A yapping, hairy, hound-dog pup.

To a frog he was a horrible sight
And he gave our frog a terrible fright.
He leaped into the pond and, to his surprise,
Found he could jump rather well for his size;
And from that day on, I'm glad to say,
He joined in all the games that pond frogs play,
Not caring at all if he lost or won,
Just so happy at last to be part of the fun.
Some little frogs are not proud you see
And they flop about quite merrily,
Not caring at all if they come in last,
Or whether they swim slow or fast.
They are the ones who learn through play
And, because they like it, they win one day,"
Said Elfree looking very wise.
I glanced at him in some surprise.
"I know that you too can be a proud little elf."
"Yes, and I make things hard for myself."
So we went looking for seeds around the pond
And found some on a ferny frond.

So that's how it's done!

Love,

Gran

Dear children

"Elves love words," said Elfree today
As he sat on his box to watch me play.
He thinks when I'm painting it's playtime for me.
I tell him it's work, but he doesn't agree.
"Words are colourful, musical, funny and sad.
Some make you thoughtful and some make you glad.
Musical words make sounds like splish-splash
Or thump, snip or tinkle, bang, whip and crash.
Di', Zandy, Liam, and Andy too,
Are beautiful shades of red, yellow and blue.
Long words like willow and window and weary,
Waiting and winter, are not very cheery.
I prefer words that end up in 'ink'.
Words I can skip to, like link, think and pink.
I also like words that rhyme with thank,
Except for a few like spank and stank."
And so he went on, my little elf friend.
Talking about words and how they end.
Then he said, "Will you write this story down
For your grandchildren in Australia? It's about a clown."
So I put my brush down and stopped work for a while.
Perhaps a clown story would make us all smile.
Then our elf asked me a peculiar thing.
"Do you like bees? The ones that sting."
"Yes," I replied, "I've always liked bees.
And I like their buzz in the flowers and trees."

"Then I can tell you this story of an African bee
Who lived in a hive in an old hollow tree.
His full name was *Fred Bee of Comb and Wild Honey*
And he was one of those folk who find everything
funny.

He did crazy things to make other bees smile
And was called 'Freddie The Fool' after a while.
He buzzed around the fat hippopotamus
And sat on the horn of the black rhinoceros.

He flew through the jaws of the crocodile
And rested on the cobra's hood for a while.
He rode on the tusks of the wild wort-hogs
And worried the Yellow African dogs;

And when they roared and snapped and hissed
He'd fly into the air and say, 'You missed!'
But the animal he liked most to tease,
Was Aap van Skalkwyk the dominee;*
For there was something about his pious look
And dark black suit and big black book
And the way he fixed his stony stare
On the other poor people gathered there
That made Freddie The Fool, the naughty bee,
Play his Sunday trick on the dominee.
He'd wait till the parson would start to tell
His congregation they were bound for hell,

* A strict preacher who had no
confidence in the goodness of people

Then Freddie would settle on his nose
And buzz his wings and dig in his toes,
Then the dominee would give himself a blow
That gave his nose a rosy glow
And knock his glasses to the floor,
While Freddie flew laughing out of the door.
Now bees are very hard-working folk
And have no time for silly jokes,
So Freddie was taken before Her Serene
And Most Royal Highness – The Queen.
There was Freddie, all alone;
Except for The Queen on her honeycomb throne.

'Now Freddie,' she said. 'Why are you here
And not collecting honey from somewhere out there?'
And begging the pardon of his most Royal Queen,
Freddie told her how naughty he had been.
The Queen listened to Freddie right the way through
Then said, 'I think I should be cross with you.

It's not the job of the honey bee
To plague the animals that you see,
But I do feel I must now go in search
Of a new hive, so show me this church.'
And that is how it came to be
That the following Sunday the bees left the tree,

And swarmed into the dominee's lair
Frightening the people out of there.
The church belongs to the bees today
And the children are happy because now they can play.
The last I heard of Freddie The Fool,
Was that he was showing the princess
around the school."

Elfree was pleased that he made me smile. He hopes you will smile too.

Love,

Dear children

Today we went looking for the monster you thought you saw living in the bay and this is what happened. I've written it the way Elfree talks because he helped me write the letter to you and he doesn't feel comfortable talking in prose, which is ordinary writing with no rhyming words. I said:

"Let's wander down the hill today
And go and look across the bay.
Zandy thinks a monster's living there
And I promised him when I got here
That on a sunny day or moonlight night
I'd go and see if he is right."
"What kind of monster? Did he say?"
"A large water monster in the bay
Although I'm not sure, I must confess,
I think it's like the monster of Loch Ness.
Let's just go and see what we can see;
It would be great. Don't you agree?
If we found a Nessie in the bay.
People would come from miles away."
So off we went, wishing you were here,
He said that you would have no fear,
For Elfree was just a little scared
And thought that you would be prepared
To calm a monster if it got mad

And he would have liked to hold your hand.
So watching from the shore today
We searched the waters of the bay
For the slightest shadow, ripple or swish
But all we saw were crabs and fish.
Then a head appeared above the waves,
With large brown eyes and a distant gaze
And wet grey fur, as sleek as steel,
But it turned out to be a seal.
"Perhaps if we call to it loud and clear
Zandy's monster will appear."
So we called, and our call was carried away,
Over the water, over the bay,
On the wind which blew across waves and sky,
And Elfree was right, it did hear our cry;

For after our call a shape was seen
Like a grey and ghostly submarine.
It swam towards us, silent and grey,
As we stood spellbound at the edge of the bay,
Then slowly it lifted its enormous head
Which was smooth and shiny, like wet lead,
And we felt as we watched him
that the monster knew
Great love and joy, and suffering too
And as it gazed on us we lost our fear,
For in his huge eye was a silent prayer
That man would learn to love his kind
And with his heart and with his mind
Know that never once had they
Hurt men or elves in any way;
Then, with a flick of his giant tail,
He turned and left, that great blue whale,

And silently we both watched him go,
Wanting to talk to him, to let him know
We understood and loved him too,
Zandy's gentle monster from the ocean blue.
Then he turned at the entrance of the bay
And, like a sigh on the wind, we heard him say,
"A wonderful gift is your love for me
That will be felt by all whales in the sea.
Farewell, I must follow an ocean trail."
And he was gone with a wave of his mighty tail.

As we walked slowly up the hill
Elfree said nothing, which is strange for him.
Then, nearing home, he asked if we might
Write to you this very night;
So this is what we're doing now
And Elfree says he'd like you to know
That after seeing the great blue whale
He'll never be nervous of monsters again.
And would you all be his human friends?
Remembering that friendships have no end.

    Love,

Gran

Dear children

I hear you had a lot of rain. Well Elfree says elves use rain and mist like a doorway into our world, so when it's misty it's easier for humans and elves to see each other. If you do see an elf, greet it politely.

Our little elf made a fool of himself; at least so he thought, and was suffering from embarrassment when I last saw him. He told me his story and I've written it down for you.

"Have you ever felt like an absolute fool,
Embarrassed and shy and very uncool?"
Asked Elfree today as we walked together
Over the hills and through the heather.
"Of course," I said. "Everyone, willy-nilly,
Sometimes feels foolish and very silly."
"Well I'm a very proud young elf
And I don't like making a fool of myself."
"I know just how you feel," I said then,
"But it will pass and you'll feel right again.
But why the question?" I asked my elf.
"Last night I made a complete fool of myself!"

That he felt silly, I think you'll agree,
When you hear the story he told to me.

"Sometimes when the full moon rises
We elves give aviation prizes
To all nocturnal flying things,
Like moths and glow-worms
and ants with wings.
The prizes go to those who try
To reach the moon and touch the sky,
Or to those who show the brightest light
Or swoop and turn for our delight.
It's a merry night and all have fun
And I am usually the one
Who writes the lists of all the names
Of those who join the flying games;
And this I was doing before the light
Was stolen away by the night,
When along came a mouse with a cheeky face
And said his cousin was entering the race
To the moon, taking place that very night,
So would I please write his name down for the flight.

To please the mouse with his silly story
I wrote down the name of his cousin Rory.
Then I laughed out loud and slapped my knee
And called my friends to joke with me.
'Tonight we'll all be proud to be
A part of flying history,
About to be made,' I said with a grin,
'By a mouse called Rory James O'Flynn.'
And we laughed to think a mouse was trying
To write a new chapter in the story of flying.
Then the cheeky mouse, with a cheeky grin,
Said he'd take bets that his cousin would win,
From everyone who didn't believe the story
That his beloved country cousin Rory
Could fly faster and higher into the air
Than the strongest flying insect there.

Well, you've guessed what happened after that,
His cousin Rory was a bat.
Of course he'd been right all along,
But I wished all the same that he'd been wrong!"
"I feel so foolish," said Elfree then.
"I don't want to return to the elfin glen."
Then I took his small hand into mine
As we walked along in the warm sunshine.

"There is something we humans can teach you elves,
And that is to learn to laugh at yourselves."
"Teach me that," said Elfree. "Teach me now."
"Just join in the laughter, that is how.
No one will mock you if you admit
That you were a rather silly twit.
What can they say to you after that?
The mean ones may remind you O'Flynn was a bat,
But the mean ones are not your friends, are they?
So go back to the glen to have fun and play."

And that is exactly what he did.

Love,

Dear children

Elfree is off to visit his cousin, but before he left he asked me to write this story for you.

Before I begin the story I should explain that when elves want their listeners to see something clearly they draw a ring on the ground and put whatever it is they want you to see into it. In your imagination you then see it quite well.

"Here is a story for your grandsons and Di,
Of a place now past and a time gone by;
Of a queen and a king from each of our planes
Who tried to join the two domains
Of men and elves, so that we could share
Our talents and knowledge and love and care
For the Earth we wish to preserve and protect
From greed, destruction and neglect.
The story I wish to tell to them now
Is of Arthur Pendragon, whom you all know,
But he was also, in part, an elfin king,
And his mother I now put into the ring.

She was an elfin queen, worthy and gentle,
And she wore the famous elfin mantle:
A sleeveless cloak of gold and green
With jewelled leaf clasped between
And, woven into the cloak in red,
Finest gold and silver thread,
The kingdom's crest of wave and sword
And, written beneath, the fairy word:

The meaning is to know your worth
And, with this knowledge, serve the earth.
Our elfin queen joined an earthly king.
I now put Uther into the ring.
Arthur's father, strong and true,
Noble and wise and gentle too.
Their child was born on the first of May
And as a boy he was sent away
To forge a link and create a spot
That would later be known as Camelot.
This was their child who was to be king.
I now put Arthur into the ring.

There were enemies then of men and elves
Who wanted power for themselves;
They wished to destroy the child who'd be
The window through which men could see
Into elfin lands which were fading fast
From the sight of men in those times past.
So Arthur, a child lost to his mother,
His father gone, no true sister or brother,
Was left in the care of a kindly knight
And hidden away from his enemies' sight
By taking all rank and privilege away
And not telling the child he'd be king one day;
By disguising him as a lad of the court
And giving him the name of Wort.
And now I put Merlin into the ring:
An elf who taught the future king.
His task, this elf so old and wise,
Was to tutor Wort from the age of five
And, recognising the wisdom of wave
and sword,
Arthur listened to his every word.

He learned that to be wise you have to be kind
And freedom is how you use your mind.
Loyalty is earned, not given to you,
And laughter has healing powers too;
How you honour others is how well you'll lead
And the wisdom of ages is yours if you read.
By becoming an owl he learned to fly
And saw no borders from the sky.
And all this time Merlin was preparing
For the day he and Arthur would be merging,
For it was the only way then
That Arthur could leave the place of men
And walk with ease through fairy places
And learn the lore of the elfin races.
It was at this time that a great sword
Was fashioned by dwarves in a faerie forge;
And I now put Excalibur into the ring,
A sword made by dwarves for a future king.
The people of England were given the word.
Only a king could own the sword,

And the sword was placed in the heart of a stone
For the man who would remove it and be
given the throne.
Many men tried – wise, strong and old,
But none could loosen its stony hold
Until Arthur tried, as a young man
And the sword was released into his hand.
What happened to Excalibur and Arthur then
Is better known to you in the world of men.
We heard of his table of loyal knights
Who fought for truth and might for right.
We heard too of his enemies, dark and black,
Who fought to bring the old ways back,
And always, as into battle he'd ride,
Excalibur was with him by his side.
At the end of his life it was returned by Arthur
Into the hand of his elfin mother,
Who used a lake to form a way
Through which to reach it that last day;
And now it rests, so smooth and sharp,
In the Elfin halls where stands the harp

That will be heard once again to play
When the veil is cut and we meet one day.
The mortal side of Arthur died
But elves were waiting at his side
And moved his body out to sea,
From his earthly battles he was free.
Arthur the elf and human king;
I now put history into the ring:
It's not the winning or losing or how he died,
But the wonderful story of how he tried.
The history of battles lost and won,
Into our tapestries are spun,
But what gives them colour and makes them glow
Is the endeavour and courage that brave folk show."

Did you know that Excalibur was made from
steel from a meteorite and that elves believe
that this gives it a special and magical
quality?

Love,

Gran

Dear children

Today while Elfree and I were strolling in the mist, which he said elves liked, I asked him why he was always so happy and liked everything, except hob goblins, and he replied: "We learn to to be happy, it's very important for elves." Then he explained:

"Elves don't get colds, hay-fever or 'flu',
Or coughs or mumps like humans do.
Their backs and necks and heads don't get sore
But just as serious, perhaps even more,
Are the things that make elves feel bad,
Which are; bad temper, bad words or feeling sad.
Elves can't help things grow if they're feeling poorly,
All plants in their keeping will fade and grow droopy
So it's very important that elves feel good;
Perhaps it's also important that humans should?
Happiness is taught in all elfin classes
And a grade 'A' in joy is the best of passes.
Pinned to the board of the classroom tree,
These rules on happiness you will see:
Rule one is to be liked by your fellow elves,
That makes you feel good and like yourselves,
And there, written in beautiful letters of gold,
Is how to be liked by young and old.
This golden list in the classroom tree
Is called by young elves the "To be's".

To be easy going and relaxed in your way,
To be cheerful and joyful and happy at play,
To be gentle with everyone, especially babies,
To be polite to all and bow to ladies,
To be forgiving of others and yourselves,
To encourage and praise smaller elves,
To be kind and loving, even to pests,
To be merry and happy and try your best.
The second rule makes you feel pleased inside
And to all we elves it's our daily guide;
Like doing a dance of joy every day
And enjoying work as well as play,
And greeting everyone with a smile
And doing a good turn once in a while,
And telling the truth, if the truth is kind,
And to know life is good and keep it in mind.
If you do all these things you will never feel blue
But bright and friendly and happy and true.

I asked Elfree if he did all the things he had learned and he said "Nooooo..." Sometimes he got mean and cross with other elves and things would go way down into gloom and bad feelings and his plants would wilt and droop, but he always had his golden list and it would help him back to happiness. I thought, maybe it would help humans; all except the bowing to ladies, which really isn't done anymore. It would look funny, don't you think?

Of course, being your grandmother and loving you so much, I would like to give you happiness in a parcel if I could, but it's not something someone else can give you; it is something you have to learn for yourself. Well that's good too, for once you have made it your own you can't lose it. Can you?

Love,

Gran